marla frazee

THE FARMER AND THE CIRCUS

Beach Lane Books

NEW YORK · LONDON · TORONTO · SYDNEY · NEW DELHI

For the stars that hold our wishes

BEACH LANE BOOKS
An imprint of Simon & Schuster Children's Publishing Division
1230 Avenue of the Americas, New York, New York 10020
© 2021 by Marla Frazee
Book design by Marla Frazee and Lauren Rille © 2021 by Simon & Schuster, Inc.
All rights reserved, including the right of reproduction in whole or in part in any form.
BEACH LANE BOOKS and colophon are trademarks of Simon & Schuster, Inc.
For information about special discounts for bulk purchases, please contact Simon & Schuster Special Sales
at 1-866-506-1949 or business@simonandschuster.com.
The Simon & Schuster Speakers Bureau can bring authors to your live event. For more information or to book an event,
contact the Simon & Schuster Speakers Bureau at 1-866-248-3049 or visit our website at www.simonspeakers.com.
The illustrations for this book were rendered in black Prismacolor pencil and gouache.
Manufactured in China
0121 SCP
First Edition
10 9 8 7 6 5 4 3 2 1
Library of Congress Cataloging-in-Publication Data
Names: Frazee, Marla, author, illustrator.
Title: The farmer and the circus / Marla Frazee.
Description: First edition. | New York : Beach Lane Books, [2021] | Series: [The farmer books ; 3] | Audience: Ages 4-8. |
Audience: Grades 2-3. |
Summary: A wordless picture book in which the farmer visits the little clown and the monkey, and meets the rest of the circus family.
Identifiers: LCCN 2020030297 (print) | LCCN 2020030298 (ebook) | ISBN 9781534446212 (hardcover) | ISBN
9781534446229 (ebook)
Subjects: CYAC: Farmers—Fiction. | Circus—Fiction. | Clowns—Fiction. | Monkeys—Fiction. | Stories without words.
Classification: LCC PZ7.F866 Fap 2021 (print) | LCC PZ7.F866 (ebook) | DDC [E]—dc23
LC record available at https://lccn.loc.gov/2020030297
LC ebook record available at https://lccn.loc.gov/2020030298